River Boy: The Story of Mark Twain Copyright © 2003 by William Anderson Illustrations copyright © 2003 by Dan Andreasen
Printed in the U.S.A. All rights reserved. www.harperchildrens.com Library of Congress Cataloging-in-Publication Data
Anderson, William   River boy : the story of Mark Twain / by William Anderson ; illustrated by Dan Andreasen.—1st ed.
p. cm.   ISBN 0-06-028400-5 — ISBN 0-06-028401-3 (lib. bdg.)   1. Twain, Mark, 1835–1910—Childhood and youth—
Juvenile literature. 2. Authors, American—19th century—Biography—Juvenile literature. 3. Pilots and pilotage—Mississippi
River Region—Biography—Juvenile literature. 4. River life—Mississippi River—Juvenile literature. 5. Mississippi River—
Juvenile literature. [1. Twain, Mark, 1835–1910. 2. Authors, American.] I. Andreasen, Dan, ill.   II. Title. PS1332.A53
2002 00-044865 818'.409—dc21 CIP [B] AC Typography by Elynn Cohen 1 2 3 4 5 6 7 8 9 10 ❖ First Edition

River Boy

The Story of Mark Twain

By William Anderson

Illustrated by Dan Andreasen

HarperCollins Publishers

"Ste-e-e-eamboat's a-comin'!"

Whenever that cry sounded through the streets of Hannibal, Missouri, most everyone noticed. The great steamboats chugging up and down the Mississippi River were always filled with interesting things—new goods for the stores, letters from far-off places, and people Hannibal had never seen. No one knew who or what might come off that boat.

A curly-headed boy named Sam Clemens watched from a tree near the water's edge as the big boat docked on the riverbank. Like his friends, Sam dreamed of being a steamboat pilot.

The Clemens house was a block from the river. Sam's mother was fun-loving and patient—even when Sam played pranks like teasing the family cat. Sam's father was called Judge Clemens. He worked as a lawyer, a storekeeper, and a justice of the peace. There was not much money to be made in the frontier town, but Sam and his brothers and sister knew there would always be a good warm meal for them when they raced home from school or play.

Sam's family hadn't always lived in Hannibal. He was born in another Missouri town called Florida. His mother told him that when he was born, on November 30, 1835, a long, dazzling streak of white light traveled across the nighttime sky.

People peered through their windows to see Halley's
Comet shoot through the dark. They would have to wait
seventy-six more years to see that comet again.

Inside the Clemens house, though, the important event
was the arrival of a tiny, pale, redheaded baby named Sam.

Sam grew up tough, wiry, and full of mischief. He and his friends explored the dark, spooky passages of McDowell's Cave in a quest for pirate treasure. They sampled watermelons from farmers' fields and had seed-spitting contests. The river was always nearby for swimming, fishing, and borrowing boats to row to islands in the middle of the Mississippi.

Sam loved being the center of attention. When measles made the rounds of most of Hannibal's children, Sam wanted them, too. He hopped into bed with a sick friend, and by the next day, he came down with the measles. Sam got lots of attention, but he barely lived to enjoy it.

When he was older, Sam's mother told him that he had given her *much* more trouble than the other children in the family. "I suppose you were afraid I wouldn't live," Sam joked.

"No," she replied. "Afraid you *would*!"

Once Sam nearly drowned while swimming in the deep waters of the Mississippi, so his parents told him not to swim there. But he couldn't resist the strong, wild river, and his parents caught him. As a punishment, Sam had to whitewash the tall board fence near his house one sunny Saturday. To him it seemed *miles* long.

As he brushed the dripping whitewash over the boards, Sam spied a friend nearby. He had an idea. He pretended that whitewashing was great fun, and it was not a job to be trusted to just anyone. Soon his friend begged to help, and before long neighborhood boys were waiting in line to paint the Clemenses' fence.

At school Sam was a restless student. He was the school's best speller, but his real talent seemed to be getting into trouble. One day Sam led a group of boys on an "adventure." They skipped school and rowed to an island in the Mississippi. They were mighty hunters for the day—fishing, digging turtles' eggs, and building campfires.

While exploring the island, they made a shocking discovery—the body of a runaway slave floating in the water.

Another time, Sam saw slaves chained together, waiting to be sent farther south to work on plantations. He never forgot that terrible scene and wondered why *all* people could not be as free as he was.

Just before Sam turned twelve, his father died. Sam knew he must quit school and help his mother. He went to work on the *Hannibal Courier* newspaper as a printer's apprentice. His work included delivering the paper, setting type, and running the printing press. He liked words so much that he wrote three stories himself for the paper. Sam's favorite part of his job was reading the news on the telegraph wire. He learned about the Mexican War of 1846 to 1848 and the world far beyond Hannibal.

When Sam turned seventeen, he was itching to have his own adventures. He was a good printer and could write news stories, too, so he boarded a steamboat for St. Louis to work for a newspaper. When he had earned a little money, he was off again! He worked as a printer in New York and Philadelphia before returning to Hannibal.

Sam had a bold dream. He wanted to explore the faraway Amazon River in South America. He had no money for the trip, but one day a gust of wind blew a fifty-dollar bill his way. It nearly hit him in the face! He took it as a sign and used the money to board a steamboat headed south.

The hiss of the steam and the call of the whistle on the Mississippi River tugged at Sam's heart. Sam decided he could see the Amazon another time. He talked the steamboat pilot, Horace Bixby, into teaching him how to navigate the river.

Learning to be a steamboat pilot was not easy. Sam had to memorize all the shallow waters and the shifts and changes and dangerous sandbars of the mighty Mississippi. He filled an entire notebook with information he needed to know about the 1,200 miles of the river from New Orleans to St. Louis. Finally he earned his pilot's license.

Leadsmen on steamboats measured the depth of the river by lowering a rope into the water. They called back their measurements, or "marks," to the pilot. Twelve feet deep was "mark twain." Any shallower and the steamboat was in danger of getting stuck. Sam later started signing his stories "Mark Twain." With his fondness for stirring up trouble and for river life, it seemed like just the right name for him.

"I seemed to be perched on a mountain," Sam said when he described his days in the steamboat pilot house, watching the river flow by. He wanted to follow the river for the rest of his life. But in 1861 the Civil War between the North and South ended Sam's plans. River travel was no longer safe, so Sam quit his job on the Mississippi and headed for the Wild West.

Now Sam had "mining fever." He planned to get rich by mining silver and gold. In Nevada Territory, Sam saw men find fortunes and lose them. He never struck gold himself, but he started writing about "goldbug fever" for the *Territorial Enterprise* newspaper, signing his articles as "Mark Twain" for the first time.

Sam liked swapping tales with miners. His own story "The Celebrated Jumping Frog of Calaveras County" made everyone laugh. When it was published in 1865 in newspapers all over America, people were eager for more stories by Mark Twain.

Sam Clemens had finally struck gold—with his story.

Sam Clemens, the river boy from Hannibal, was the talk of the country; he knew how to make people laugh until their sides hurt. He started giving hilarious lectures all over. The advertising posters announced:

The doors open at 7.
The trouble begins at 8.

Even with his success, Sam was still restless. He decided to sail to Europe, and he wrote of his adventures in the book *The Innocents Abroad.* The book was a great success, but more important to Sam was a beautiful girl he had met named Olivia Langdon.

In 1870 Sam and Livy were married. They first settled in Buffalo, New York, but soon moved to Hartford, Connecticut.

Livy often laughed at Sam's silly ways and called him "Youth" because he acted like a boy. Sam continued to

write his stories. Livy read his manuscripts and made helpful suggestions.

The Clemens house was a happy place. Sam and Livy soon had a bustling family with three daughters, Susy, Clara, and Jean. They also had a family dog named Hash.

In 1874 Sam built a fanciful house for his family
in Hartford, Connecticut. It had nineteen rooms, five
balconies, and a special chimney just for Santa Claus. The
top floor even resembled a pilot house on a Mississippi
River steamboat. This is where Sam wrote one of his
best-loved books, *The Adventures of Tom Sawyer.*

The characters in *Tom Sawyer* were based on people Sam
had known back in Hannibal. Aunt Polly was like his own

mother. Sam's brother Henry became the well-behaved Sid. His first girlfriend, Laura Hawkins, was transformed into Tom's girlfriend, Becky Thatcher.

Tom Sawyer was so popular that Sam wrote a sequel called The Adventures of Huckleberry Finn. It took him eight years to write. Huckleberry Finn was also based on Sam's memories of growing up along the banks of the Mississippi River.

Sam, known to the public as Mark Twain, was one of America's most famous men. People everywhere smiled when they saw him walking along the streets in his white suit. He gave more than one thousand lectures that made people howl with laughter over his tales of life on the Mississippi. Sam was so well known that a letter addressed simply to "Mark Twain, United States" reached him with no trouble.

When Sam was in his seventies, he moved to a house he called Stormfield, in Redding, Connecticut. The children of Redding loved the white-haired author who told them his "string of yarns." He knew how important libraries were for children, so he gave one to the town.

Sam once told his daughter Clara that he wished to leave the world just as he had entered it—with Halley's Comet. On April 21, 1910, when the comet once again appeared, Sam Clemens died.

All over the world, people who loved the rambunctious river boy and author watched the comet's long tail of light streaking across the sky. To them, it belonged to one of America's greatest storytellers, Mark Twain.

The Life of
Samuel Clemens/Mark Twain

1835	Born in Florida, Missouri, November 30.
1839	Clemens family moves to Hannibal, Missouri.
1847	Sam's father, John M. Clemens, dies.
1848–53	Works as printer's apprentice on Hannibal newspapers.
1853–57	Works for newspapers in St. Louis; New York; Philadelphia; Muscatine and Keokuk, Iowa; and Cincinnati.
1857–61	Works as a Mississippi steamboat pilot.
1862–67	Works as a newspaper and magazine reporter out west.
1865	The *New York Saturday Press* publishes short story "The Celebrated Jumping Frog of Calaveras County."
1868	First lecture tour.
1869	*The Innocents Abroad* is published.
1870	Marries Olivia Langdon. Edits newspaper, *Buffalo Express*. Son, Langdon, is born.
1872	*Roughing It* is published. Daughter Susy is born. Langdon dies.
1873	*The Gilded Age*, written with Charles Dudley Warner, is published.
1874	Daughter Clara is born. *The Gilded Age* becomes a successful stage play.